For my beautiful River . . . Love you hoo

ORCHARD BOOKS

First published in Great Britain in hardback in 2016 by The Watts Publishing Group

First published in paperback in 2017 • 1 3 5 7 9 10 8 6 4 2 • Text and illustrations © Rachel Bright, 2016

The moral rights of the author have been asserted • All rights reserved

A CIP catalogue record for this book is available from the British Library

HB ISBN 978 1 40833 169 9 • PB ISBN 978 1 40833 170 5

Printed and bound in China

MIX
Paper from responsible sources
FSC® C104740

FSC
www.fsc.org

Orchard Books • An imprint of Hachette Children's Group • Part of The Watts Publishing Group Limited

Carmelite House, 50 Victoria Embankment, London EC4Y 0DZ

An Hachette UK Company • www.hachette.co.uk • www.hachettechildrens.co.uk

LoVe you
hOo

LoVe you hOo

Rachel Bright

ORCHARD

Cuddle up now, little one,
Let's snuggle wing-to-wing.
Are you feeling safe and warm?
Ok then, let's begin . . .

There's something I **MUST** tell you
Before you close your eyes.
I want to
Woo-**hoo-hoo** it

So it fills the **starry** skies.

Ever since you hatched, you see,
You set my world **alight!**
With you **hoo-hoo**,

Each day becomes
so colourful and bright.

You make life feel like sunshine,
No matter what the weather.

And **ANYTHING** is possible,
As long as we're together.

I'll show you what I've come to know,
And try to teach you things.
Perhaps I'll give a gentle nudge
To help you find your wings.

But... you teach me too,
hoo-hoo,
To look through different eyes.
Yes, little ones can often be
So very, VERY wise.

HELLO!

We'll never stop exploring,
There's so much to see and do.
Now you're here, there's
ALWAYS more

I'm looking forWard to.

And if things don't
quite go to plan,

If there are scrapes . . .

Oh, with you life is SO wonderful.
You're times-a-million GREAT!
And everything's a piece of cake,

Whatever's on Our plate!

So here are all my kisses,
And another one for sure.
Some hugs and tickles too,

hoo-hoo.

And, then,
perhaps some . . .

Yes . . .
there's something
I MUST tell you.
This thing
I HAVE to say,

It flips my heart quite upside-down
In just the nicest way.

You see . . .

Whoever you are going to be . . .

Whatever you may DO . . .

Wherever you may choose to fly ...